Great Expectations

BY

Charles Dickens

EDITED BY

Philip Page and Marilyn Pettit

ILLUSTRATED BY

Philip Page

Published in association with
The
Basic Skills
Agency

Hodder & Stoughton

A MEMBER OF THE HODDER HEADLINE GROUP

Orders: please contact Bookpoint Ltd, 130 Milton Park, Abingdon, Oxon OX14 4SB.
Telephone: (44) 01235 827720, Fax: (44) 01235 400454. Lines are open from 9.00–6.00,
Monday to Saturday, with a 24 hour message answering service. You can also order
through our website www.hodderheadline.co.uk

British Library Cataloguing in Publication Data
A catalogue record for this title is available from The British Library

ISBN 0 340 87161 X

First published 2003
Impression number   10 9 8 7 6 5 4 3 2 1
Year   2007 2006 2005 2004 2003

Text Copyright © 2003 Philip Page and Marilyn Pettit
Illustrations Copyright © 2002 Philip Page

Cover illustration by Dave Smith
Typeset by Fakenham Photosetting Ltd, Fakenham, Norfolk
Printed in Great Britain for Hodder & Stoughton Educational, a division of Hodder
Headline, 338 Euston Road, London NW1 3BH by J.W. Arrowsmith, Bristol.

Contents

About the story

Great Expectations is often described as a *sensation novel*. It was one of Dickens's most popular novels.

It has lots of ingredients that people enjoy reading about:

• crime, revenge, violence, threats

as well as:

• kind-hearted people, love, loyalty and friendship.

It also has memorable characters:

• Miss Havisham and Magwitch.

When you have finished reading the book, decide why it is sometimes referred to as a *sensation novel*.

Which character is the one you will remember long after you have finished reading this novel and why?

Cast of characters

'Pip' (Philip Pirrip)
age 8   age 21   age 32

Joe Gargery
A blacksmith.

Mrs Joe
Joe's wife and Pip's sister.

Biddy
A village teacher.

Uncle Pumblechook
Joe's uncle.

Mr Wopsle
A church clerk who
becomes an actor.

Orlick
A man who
works for Joe.

Miss Havisham
An eccentric wealthy lady.

Estella
Miss Havisham's
adopted child.

Abel Magwitch
A convict.

Mr Jaggers
A London lawyer.

Wemmick
His clerk.

Molly
His housekeeper.

Matthew Pocket
Miss Havisham's cousin.

Herbert Pocket
His son.

Bentley Drummle
A young man Pip
meets in London.

Compeyson
A convict.

Pip begins his story. He meets a frightening stranger in the graveyard. He is so scared he agrees to steal some things for him.

My father's family name being Pirrip, and my Christian name Philip, my infant tongue could make nothing longer than Pip. So, I called myself Pip. I never saw my father or mother.

Ours was the marsh country, down by the river.

wittles (victuals) – food and drink

Joe was sitting alone in the kitchen.

Mrs Joe has been out looking for you, Pip ...

... and she's got Tickler with her.

She's coming! Get behind the door.

Where have you been?

Only to the churchyard.

You'll drive me to the churchyard one of these days.

She set the tea-things, cutting our bread-and-butter.

Though I was hungry, I dared not eat. I must have something for my dreadful acquaintance and the still more dreadful young man. I put my bread-and-butter down the leg of my trousers.

Joe saw that my bread-and-butter was gone.

Pip, old chap! You'll do yourself a mischief. It'll stick somewhere. You can't have **chawed** it.

What's the matter now? Been bolting his food, has he?

You come and **be dosed**.

chawed – chewed

be dosed – take some medicine

3

It was Christmas Eve and I had to stir the pudding for the next day.

Hark! Was that guns, Joe?

There was a **conwict off** last night. They fired warning of him. And now they're firing warning of another.

Who's firing?

From the Hulks.

What's Hulks?

Prison-ships. People are put in the Hulks because they murder, rob and do all sorts of bad things.

Now get to bed!

At the first faint dawn of morning, I stole some bread, some cheese, about half a jar of mincemeat, some brandy, a meat bone and a pork pie.

conwict – convict
off – escaped

I got a file from among Joe's tools …

… and ran for the misty marshes.

4

Pip gives the stranger the food and the file and then runs off scared.

Pip is even more worried when his sister goes to fetch the pork pie he has stolen; and a party of soldiers turns up.

We were to have a superb dinner its being Christmas Day. The dinner hour was half-past one. I opened the door to the company:

... Mr Wopsle ... Mr and Mrs Hubble ... and Uncle Pumblechook.

We dined on these occasions in the kitchen.

You must taste, to finish with, a delicious savoury pork pie.

I could bear no more ...

... and ran for my life ...

... into a party of soldiers on our doorstep.

I am on a chase in the name of the King, and I want the blacksmith.

We have had an accident with these and the lock of one of 'em goes wrong. Will you **throw your eye over them**?

Convicts, sergeant?

Ay! two. They're out on the marshes.

At last Joe's job was done. Joe **mustered courage** to propose that some of us should go with the soldiers and see what became of the hunt. We came out on the marshes.

I looked all about for any sign of the convicts. I could see none, I could hear none.

All of a sudden, a shout.

Murder!

Convicts! Guard! This way!

The sergeant ran in a ditch. More men went down to help and dragged out my convict and the other man.

He tried to murder me.

I took him, and giv' him up.

throw your eye over them – have a look at them
mustered courage – got up the nerve

7

Do you see what a villain he is? That's how he looked when we were tried together.

My convict looked round him for the first time and saw me. I shook my head that I might assure him of my innocence. He gave me a look that I did not understand.

All right! March!

After an hour or so we came to a rough wooden hut and a landing-place.

I wish to say something. I took some wittles, up at the village – a **dram** of liquor, and a pie.

So you're the blacksmith, are you? I'm sorry I've eat your pie.

You're welcome to it.

We don't know what you have done, but we wouldn't have you starved to death for it. Would us, Pip?

We saw him put into the boat, rowed by convicts like himself to the black Hulk lying a little way out from the shore.

dram – small amount

A year has passed since the convicts were captured. Pip chats to Joe and his sister comes home with exciting news!

Why didn't you ever go to school, Joe?

My mother and me ran away from my father several times. He'd come and then he took us home and hammered us. Which were a drawback on my learning.

When you take me in hand in my learning, Pip, Mrs Joe mustn't see what we're up to. She would not be partial to my being a scholar.

Howsumever, here's the clock working himself up to strike Eight and she's not home yet!

We went to the door to listen.

If this boy an't grateful this night, he never will be.

Miss Havisham wants this boy to go and play there.

Uncle Pumblechook has offered to take him to-morrow morning.

I was soaped and towelled, and thumped and put into clean linen.

Howsumever – however

9

Pip meets Miss Havisham and Estella who live in a very strange house.

Ten o'clock came and we started for Miss Havisham's house, which was of old brick, and dismal, and had a great many iron bars to it. Some of the windows had been walled up.

After ringing the bell a window was raised.

What name?

Pumblechook. This is Pip.

Come in, Pip.

We went into the house by a side door – the passages were dark! We went up a staircase. At last we came to a door.

Go in.

After you, miss.

Don't be ridiculous, boy; I am not going in.

I knocked and was told to enter.

In an armchair, with an elbow resting on the table and her head leaning on that hand, sat the strangest lady I have ever seen, or shall ever see. She was dressed in white and had bridal flowers in her hair. But everything was faded and yellow. Her figure had shrunk to skin and bone.

Come nearer; let me look at you. Come close.

I should like to go home.

You shall go soon. Play the game out.

Come again after six days. Estella, take him down. Let him have something to eat.

Wait here, boy.

She came back and gave me bread and meat as if I were a dog. I was so hurt that tears started to my eyes.

The girl looked at me with delight – and left me.

I got rid of my feelings by kicking the brewery wall.

I was soon **in spirits** to look about me.

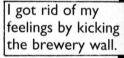

in spirits – in the mood

It was a deserted place, no pigeons in the dove-cot, no horses in the stable, no pigs in the sty. Behind the brewery was a garden overgrown with tangled weeds. I saw Estella approaching with the keys, to let me out.

Why don't you cry?

I don't want to.

She laughed, pushed me out and locked the gate. I set off on the four-mile walk to our forge.

Pip decides to become educated! He also meets someone who gives him a fright.

The idea occurred to me a morning or two later that the best step I could take towards making myself uncommon was to get out of Biddy, the teacher, everything she knew.

I mentioned to Biddy that I had a particular reason for wishing to get on in life.

There was a public house in the village. Joe liked sometimes to smoke his pipe there.

I received orders from my sister to call for him on my way from school. Joe was with Mr Wopsle and a stranger.

Halloa, Pip, old chap!

The stranger looked at me.

What is it you call him?

Pip.

The strange man looked at nobody but me.

He stirred his rum with a file. Nobody but I saw.

Joe got up to go.

I've a shilling in my pocket, the boy shall have it.

He folded it in some paper, and gave it to me. In the kitchen I took out the paper – two One-Pound notes. Joe ran to restore them to their owner. The man was gone. My sister put them in an ornamental teapot.

Another visit to Miss Havisham and Pip learns more about her and her visitors. He ends up in a fight.

I returned to Miss Havisham's.

This way to-day.

Stand there, boy, till you are wanted.

There were three ladies in the room and one gentleman. They all had a **listless** and dreary air of waiting someone's pleasure.

The ringing of a distant bell interrupted the conversation.

Now, boy!

Estella stopped.

Am I pretty?

Very pretty.

Am I insulting?

Not so much as last time.

What do you think of me now? Why don't you cry again?

I'll never cry for you again.

We went upstairs and met a gentleman groping his way down. He was nothing to me, and I could have had no foresight then, that he ever would be anything to me.

How do *you* come here?

listless – tired

15

Miss Havisham sent for me, sir.

Well! Behave yourself.

We were soon in Miss Havisham's room.

Go into that opposite room and wait there till I come.

I entered the room. Every thing in it was covered with dust and mould, and dropping to pieces. I saw spiders. I heard mice too.

This is where I will be laid when I am dead. They shall come and look at me here.

A **bride-cake**. Mine!

bride-cake – wedding cake

Estella brought the three ladies and gentleman.

How well you look.

I have thought of you.

Go!

This is my birthday, Pip. They come here on the day, but they dare not refer to it.

On this day, long before you were born, this heap of decay was brought here. It and I have worn away together. The mice have gnawed at it and sharper teeth than teeth of mice have gnawed at me.

When the ruin is complete and they lay me dead, in my bride's dress on the bride's table and which will be the finished curse upon him — much the better if it is done on this day.

Let me see you two play cards.

When we had played, a day was **appointed** for my return, and I was taken down into the yard to be fed in the former dog-like manner.

I strolled into the garden. I looked in at another window and found a pale young gentleman.

Who gave you **leave** to prowl about?

Miss Estella.

appointed – chosen

leave – permission

Come and fight.

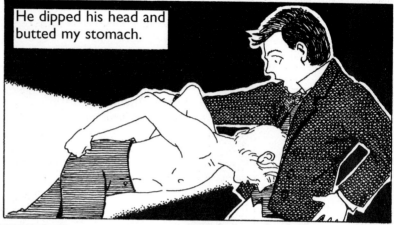

He dipped his head and butted my stomach.

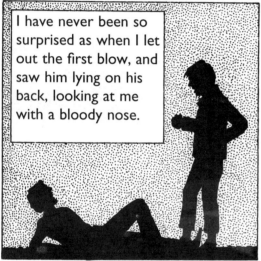

I have never been so surprised as when I let out the first blow, and saw him lying on his back, looking at me with a bloody nose.

He was on his feet **directly**.

The second greatest surprise was seeing him on his back again, looking at me out of a black eye.

You have won.

I found Estella waiting with the keys.

You may kiss me, if you like.

I kissed her cheek.

My stay lasted so long, that when I neared home Joe's furnace was flinging a path of fire across the road.

directly – immediately

Pip goes to see Miss Havisham more regularly. She helps him out with his future, but Pip has doubts.

The more I thought of the fight, the more certain it appeared that something would be done to me. However, nothing came of the late struggle.

Estella was always about, and always let me in and out. When we played at cards Miss Havisham would embrace her.

Break their hearts my pride and hope, break their hearts and have no mercy!

What could I become with these surroundings? How could my character fail to be influenced by them?

I told poor Biddy everything. Why I told her, I did not know then, though I think I know now.

One day Miss Havisham looked at me.

That blacksmith of yours. The master you were to be apprenticed to? You had better be apprenticed at once. Let him come soon, and come alone with you.

On the next day but one we walked to town. Estella opened the gate as usual.

You have reared the boy with the intention of taking him for your apprentice? Have you brought his **indentures** with you?

indentures – apprenticeship contract

19

Pip has earned a **premium** here. There are five-and-twenty guineas in this bag. Give it to your master, Pip?

Am I to come again, Miss Havisham?

No. Gargery is your master now.

In another minute we were outside the gate, and it was locked, and Estella was gone.

The Town Hall was a queer place, I thought. Here, my indentures were signed and **attested** and I was **bound**.

My sister became so excited by the twenty-five guineas that nothing would serve her but we must have a dinner out of that windfall, at the Blue Boar, and that Pumblechook must bring the Hubbles and Mr Wopsle.

I had a strong **conviction** that I should never like Joe's trade. I had liked it once, but once was not now.

premium – reward   **attested** – witnessed   **bound** – contracted
conviction – belief

Pip asks Joe for time off and this leads to trouble and another fight. He visits Miss Havisham but is disappointed.

I never breathed a murmur to Joe while my indentures lasted. It was not because I was faithful, but because Joe was faithful, that I never ran away and went for a soldier or a sailor. What I wanted, who can say?

After dark the thought would show me Estella's face in the fire …

… and I would feel more ashamed of home than ever.

Joe, I ought to make Miss Havisham a visit.

I have never thanked her. Would you give me a half-holiday?

Joe kept a **journeyman** at weekly wages whose name was Orlick.

You're not a going to favour only one of us. If young Pip has a half-holiday, do as much for Old Orlick.

Let it be a half-holiday for all.

You fool, giving holidays to idle hulkers like that.

journeyman – workman
shrew – bad-tempered woman

You're a foul **shrew**, Mother Gargery. If you was my wife I'd choke you.

What could Joe do now, but stand up to his journeyman. They went at one another. Orlick was very soon among the coal-dust, and in no hurry to come out of it.

After visiting Miss Havisham, Pip walks home to find something awful has happened!

Miss Sarah Pocket came to the gate. No Estella. Everything was unchanged, and Miss Havisham was alone.

Well, I hope you want nothing? You'll get nothing.

Come now and then; on your birthday.

Are you looking for Estella? Abroad, educating for a lady; far out of reach; prettier than ever; admired by all who see her. Do you feel that you have lost her?

When the gate was closed upon me, I felt more than ever dissatisfied with my trade and with everything.

As I was loitering along the High-street thinking what I would buy if I were a gentleman, who should come out of the bookshop but Mr Wopsle. It was dark when I set on the track home.

We came upon a man.

Halloa, Orlick. You are late.

I come behind yourself. I didn't see you, but I must have been pretty close behind you.

We came to the village past the Three Jolly Bargemen, which we were surprised to find in a state of commotion. Mr Wopsle dropped in to ask what was the matter, but came running out in a great hurry.

22

There's something wrong up at your place, Pip. Run!

Our kitchen was full of people. I became aware of my sister lying on the bare boards where she had been knocked down by a tremendous blow on the back of the head, dealt with some unknown hand.

Joe had been at the Three Jolly Bargemen to a quarter before ten. At five minutes before ten he found her struck down on the floor.

Nothing had been taken. But there was one remarkable piece of evidence on the spot.

A convict's leg-iron which had been filed.

I believed one of two persons to have **turned it to cruel account**. Either Orlick, or the strange man who had shown me the file.

My sister lay very ill in bed. Her sight was disturbed; her hearing impaired and her speech was unintelligible. We were at a loss until Biddy became part of our establishment.

My sister traced upon the slate a curious T.

Of course! It's him!

Orlick! She could only **signify** him by his hammer. I expected my sister to denounce him. I was disappointed.

turned ... account – used it as a weapon
signify – show/describe

Pip shares his feelings with Biddy.

I became conscious of a change in Biddy. She was not beautiful like Estella – but she was pleasant.

On Sunday afternoon, Biddy and I went out to the riverside.

Biddy, I want to be a gentleman.

Don't you think you are happier as you are?

Not at all. I am disgusted with my **calling** and my life.

I am sorry for that. I want you to do well.

What would it **signify** to me, being coarse and common, if nobody had told me so!

Who said it?

The beautiful young lady at Miss Havisham's.

Do you want to be a gentleman to spite her or to gain her over?

I don't know.

If it is to spite her, that might be better done by caring nothing for her words. And if it is to gain her over, I should think she was not worth gaining over.

calling – job   **signify** – matter

24

I am glad you could give me your confidence, Pip.

Biddy, I shall always tell you everything.

Till you're a gentleman.

If only I could get myself to fall in love with you – that would be the thing for me.

But you never will, you see.

When we came near the churchyard, there started up old Orlick.

Where are you two going? I'm jiggered if I don't see you home.

Don't let him come. I don't like him. He dances at me whenever he can catch my eye.

I kept an eye on Orlick after that night.

A lawyer from London brings Pip some good news which changes his life. He is to become a gentleman!

It was in the fourth year of my apprenticeship to Joe, and it was a Saturday night. At the Three Jolly Bargemen a strange gentleman came in front of the fire.

Joe Gargery? You have an apprentice known as Pip?

Here!

The stranger did not recognise me, but I recognised him as the gentleman I had met on the stairs on my second visit to Miss Havisham.

I wish to have a private conference with you two. We had better go to your place of residence.

My name is Jaggers and I am a lawyer in London.

I am instructed to communicate to him that he will come into a **handsome property**, that he be removed from his present life and from this place, and be brought up as a gentleman of great expectations.

The name of your benefactor remains a secret until the person chooses to reveal it. It may be years **hence**.

handsome property – lot of money
hence – from now

There is a sum of money for your education. There is a tutor who might suit the purpose, Mr Matthew Pocket.

You can see his son first, who is in London.

You should have some new clothes. You'll want money. Shall I leave you twenty guineas?

This day week, take a hackney-coach at the stage coach-office in London, and come straight to me.

I thanked him.

Pip's a gentleman of fortun' then, and God bless him in it!

They both congratulated me.

Joe brought out my indentures, and we put them in the fire.

I was free.

I presented myself before the tailor. I went to the hatter's; the bootmaker's and the **hosier**'s.

I ordered everything.

I went to Miss Havisham's.

I have come into good fortune, and I am grateful for it.

I have heard about it. You go to-morrow? Good-by, Pip.

And so I left my fairy godmother.

hosier – someone who sells socks and stockings

Pip arrives in London and meets an old 'enemy'. Miss Havisham's story is told.

The journey from our town to the **metropolis** was a journey of about five hours. I came into **Smithfield**. Mr Jaggers took me into his room.

He informed me what arrangements had been made for me.

I was to go to young Mr Pocket's rooms. I was told what my allowance would be.

You will find your credit good, Mr Pip.

Of course you'll go wrong somehow, but that's no fault of mine.

I asked if I could send for a coach. He said it was not worth while, I was so near my destination. Wemmick should walk round with me if I pleased. Wemmick was the clerk.

So, you were never in London before?

No. Is it a very wicked place?

You may get cheated, robbed and murdered in London. But there are plenty of people anywhere who'll do that for you.

We entered into a little square. I thought it had the most dismal trees, sparrows, cats and houses I had ever seen.

metropolis – capital city

Smithfield – a district of London

28

As I keep the cash, we shall most likely meet pretty often. Good day.

I heard footsteps on the stairs.

Mr Pip?

Mr Pocket?

Lord bless me, you're the prowling boy!

And you are the pale young gentleman!

We both burst out laughing.

You hadn't come into your good fortune at that time?

No.

I was rather on the look-out for good fortune then.

Perhaps I should have been what-you-may-called it to Estella. Engaged.

That girl's hard and **haughty** and has been brought up by Miss Havisham to wreak revenge on all the male sex.

haughty – proud

What relation is she to Miss Havisham?

Adopted.

What revenge?

Lord, don't you know? It's quite a story. My father is Miss Havisham's cousin.

Miss Havisham was a spoilt child. Her mother died when she was a baby. Her father was a brewer, very rich and very proud. So was his daughter.

She had a half-brother. He turned out altogether bad. His father disinherited him; but he softened when he was dying and left him well off.

There appeared on the scene a man who pursued Miss Havisham.

She passionately loved him.

He got great sums of money from her. My father warned her.

The marriage day was fixed. The day came but not the bridegroom. He wrote her a letter—

Which she received at twenty minutes to nine?

At which hour afterwards she stopped all the clocks. She has never since looked upon the light of day.

It has been supposed that the man acted with her half-brother, that it was a conspiracy and they shared the profits.

You said that Estella was adopted. When?

I know no more. All that I know about Miss Havisham, you know.

Pip meets his tutor. He is to be educated to make his way in the world.

On the Monday we took coach for Hammersmith.

My Pocket was glad to see me.

He introduced me to Drummle and Startop.

Drummle was the next heir but one to a **baronetcy**.

Mr Pocket knew more of my intended career than I knew myself, for he referred to his having been told by Mr Jaggers that I was not designed for any profession.

I should be well enough educated for my destiny if I could 'hold my own' with the average of young men in prosperous circumstances.

baronetcy – title

Pip dines at Mr Jaggers' home.

Have you dined with Mr Jaggers yet?

Not yet.

When you go, look at his housekeeper.

You'll see a wild beast tamed.

My guardian gave me the invitation for myself and friends which Wemmick had prepared me to receive. At six o'clock next day he conducted us to Soho to a stately house in want of painting and with dirty windows.

He seemed interested in Drummle.

I was looking at the housekeeper.

Dinner went off gaily. We took too much to drink and we talked too much.

We became **hot upon** some sneer of Drummle's that we were too free with our money. It came with a bad grace from him, to whom Startop had lent money in my presence but a week or so before.

hot upon – annoyed about

He'll be paid.

I wouldn't lend anybody a sixpence.

Gentlemen, it's half-past nine. Good night.

Pip receives a letter. Joe visits and brings news from Miss Havisham.

MY DEAR MR PIP,
I write this by request of Mr Gargery to let you know that he is going to London in company of Mr Wopsle and would be glad to see you at Barnard's Hotel Tuesday morning at 9 o'clock. Your poor sister is much the same. We talk of you every night, and wonder what you are saying and doing.
Your ever obliged and affectionate servant, Biddy

PS He wishes me to write what larks. He says you will understand.

If I could have kept him away by paying money, I certainly would have paid money.

As the time approached I should have liked to run away.

I am glad to see you, Joe.

You have that growed and that swelled, and that gentlefolked.

Your sister, she's no worse. And Biddy, she's ever right and ready. Wopsle; **he's had a drop**. He's left the Church and went into the playacting.

he's had a drop – he's gone down in the world

T'other night, Pip, Pumblechook came to me and his word were 'Miss Havisham, she wish to speak to you'.

I go to see Miss Havisham. 'Would you tell him that Estella has come home and would be glad to see him.'

I felt my face fire up.

I have now concluded, Sir.

You are not going now, Joe?

Yes I am. You and me is not two figures to be together in London. You won't find half so much fault in me if you think of me in my forge dress, with my hammer in my hand. GOD bless, Pip, old chap!

He was gone.

I must **repair** to our town the next day. I secured my place by the afternoon coach.

repair – go

34

The meeting with Estella and Miss Havisham troubles Pip.

In the morning I loitered on Miss Havisham's side of town painting brilliant pictures of her plans for me. She had adopted Estella, she had as good as adopted me, and it could not fail to be her intention to bring us together.

She was in her chair. Near her was an elegant lady.

Do you find her much changed, Pip?

Is *he* changed?

Very much.

Estella and I went into the garden.

You must know that I have no heart. If we are to be thrown much together, you had better believe it.

We went back into the house.

Do you admire her? I adopted her to be loved. I developed her into what she is.

Love her!

It sounded like a curse.

It was arranged that when Estella came to London I should meet her. I touched her and left. Far into the night, Miss Havisham's words, 'Love her!' sounded in my ears, and I said to my pillow, 'I love her!'

Estella arrives in London. Pip gets into debt and hears the news that his sister has died.

Estella seemed more beautiful than ever.

I am going to live with a lady who has the power of taking me about and showing me to people.

It is part of Miss Havisham's plans for me. I am to write to her, see her regularly and report how I go on.

I began to **contract a quantity of debt**. Herbert, too. We spent as much money as we could, and got as little for it as people could make up their minds to give us.

My dear Herbert, we are getting on badly.

One evening we heard a letter drop through the door to inform me that Mrs J Gargery had departed this life and that my attendance was requested at the **interment** on Monday next. Having written to Joe, I went down early.

We went into the churchyard, and there my sister was laid quietly in the earth.

contract ... debt – owe a lot of money **interment** – burial

Afterwards, Biddy, Joe and I had a cold dinner together.

I took an opportunity of getting into the garden with Biddy for a little talk.

It will be difficult for you to remain here now.

I have been talking to Mrs Hubble. I hope we shall be able to take some care of Mr Gargery together, until he settles down.

I am going to try to get the place of mistress in the new school nearly finished here.

Of course I shall be often down here now. I am not going to leave poor Joe alone.

Are you quite sure that you WILL come to see him often?

Early in the morning the mists were rising as I walked away. If they **disclosed** to me that I should not come back, and that Biddy was quite right – they were quite right too.

disclosed – showed

Money comes Pip's way and he decides to help Herbert without telling him.

Time went on and I **came of age**. I received a note from Wemmick informing me that Mr Jaggers would be glad if I would call upon him.

That is a bank note for five hundred pounds. It is a present to you this day.

At the rate of that sum of money **per annum** you are to live until the donor of the whole appears.

Is it likely that my patron will soon come to London?

When that person **discloses**, you and that person will settle your own affairs.

Mr Wemmick, a friend has no money. I want somehow to help him.

We found a worthy young merchant who wanted **capital** and a partner. Secret articles were signed of which Herbert was the subject. Herbert had not the least suspicion of my hand being in it.

I shall never forget the face with which he came home one afternoon.

My **expectations** had done some good to somebody.

came of age – reached the age of 21   **per annum** – a year
discloses – decides to tell you   **capital** – money
expectations – money

Pip is jealous when Bentley Drummle takes an interest in Estella.

It is impossible to turn this leaf of my life, without putting Bentley Drummle's name upon it.

Estella!

Drummle had begun to follow her, and she allowed him to do it.

At a certain Ball at Richmond, Drummle so hung about her that I resolved to speak to her.

He is a stupid fellow.

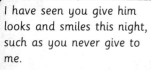

I have seen you give him looks and smiles this night, such as you never give to me.

Do you want me then to deceive and entrap you?

Do you deceive and entrap him?

Yes, and many others — all of them but you.

The convict returns and Pip is shocked at what he has to say!

It was wretched weather; stormy and wet. The day had just closed when I heard a footstep on the stair.

What do you want?

Mr Pip.

That is my name.

What is your business?

I will explain.

I knew him! My convict.

How are you living?

I've been a sheep-farmer in **the new world**.

I hope you have done well?

Wonderful well.

Have you ever seen a messenger you once sent to me? He brought me the two one-pound notes. You must let me pay them back.

the new world – Australia

He set fire to them. I began to tremble.

Could I make a guess at your income since you came of age?

As to the first figure now. Five?

There ought to have been some lawyer. As to the first letter of that lawyer's name. Would it be J?

Yes, Pip. I've made a gentleman on you! It's me wot has done it! I'm your second father. I'm the owner of a London gentleman.

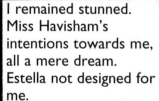

Where will you put me to sleep?

Because caution is necessary. I was sent for life. I should be hanged if took.

I remained stunned. Miss Havisham's intentions towards me, all a mere dream. Estella not designed for me.

It was for the convict that I had deserted Joe.

I could never, never, never undo what I had done.

Pip's life becomes complicated. He has to share his secret with Herbert.

I have given out that you are my uncle. You assumed some name?

Provis.

What is your real name?

Magwitch, chrisen'd Abel.

When you came, had you anyone with you?

I think there was a person.

Were you tried in London?

He nodded.

First knowed Mr Jaggers that way. And what I done is worked out and paid for!

He ate like a hungry old dog.

How long are you going to stay?

I've come for good.

There being a lodging-house in Essex-street, I was fortunate to secure the second floor for my uncle. I then went from shop to shop making purchases to change his appearance.

One morning Herbert came bursting in.

Herbert. This is – a visitor of mine!

I **recounted** the whole of the secret.

We want to know something about you.

He spread a hand on each knee and said what follows.

Twenty year ago I got acquainted wi' Compeyson, the man you see me a pounding in the ditch. His business was swindling, forging and such-like.

There was another called Arthur. Him and Compeyson had been in a bad thing with a rich lady some years afore and they'd made a pot of money by it. Arthur was dying with horrors on him.

'She's all in white,' he says, 'and over where her heart's broke – you broke it – there's blood!'

Then he lifted himself up and was dead. Me and Compeyson was both **committed for felony** and we're sentenced, him gets seven year and me fourteen. We was in the same prison ship. I escaped and I was hiding when I first see my boy! By my boy, I was giv to unnerstand as Compeyson was on the marshes. I hunted him down. I smashed his face. I was brought to trial again, and sent for life. I never heerd no more of him.

Herbert had been writing in the cover of a book. I read:

Young Havisham's name was Arthur. Compeyson is the man who professed to be Miss Havisham's lover.

recounted – told   **committed for felony** – put on trial
professed – pretended

A visit to Estella and Miss Havisham makes things worse for Pip. There is another shock in store for him when he returns to London!

I set off by the early morning coach. When we drove up to the Blue Boar, whom should I see but Bentley Drummle!

Have you been here long?

Long enough to be tired of it.

Waiter! Is that horse of mine ready? The lady won't ride today; the weather won't do. And I don't dine, because I'm going to dine at the lady's.

I went out to the old house.

I am as unhappy as you can ever have meant me to be.

I did really come here as a servant to be paid for it?

Ay, Pip.

But when I fell into the mistake I have so long remained in, you led me on? Was that kind?

Who am I that I should be kind?

the service – to help Herbert

You deeply wrong both Mr Pocket and his son Herbert. If you would spare the money to do Herbert a lasting service without his knowledge, I could show you how. I began **the service** myself.

Estella, I love you! I have loved you ever since I first saw you in this house.

She shook her head.

When you say you love me, I know what you mean, but nothing more.

Is it not true that Bentley Drummle is in town here, and pursuing you?

Why not tell you the truth? I am going to be married to him.

You will get me out of your thoughts in a week.

You are a part of myself, Estella. God bless you. God forgive you!

And so I left her. All done, all gone! I struck off to walk all the way to London. It was past midnight when the night-porter held the gate open.

Here's a note, sir.

45

I opened it and read, in Wemmick's writing:

DON'T GO HOME!

It was plain that I must see Wemmick.

Halloa, Mr Pip!

I didn't go home.

Now, Mr Pip, I heard that you at your chambers had been watched, and might be watched again.

You have heard of Compeyson? Is he living? Is he in London?

He gave me one nod.

I went to find Mr Herbert. I gave him to understand that if he was aware of anybody being about the chambers, or the neighbourhood, he had better get Tom, Jack, or Richard, out of the way.

Mr Herbert is courting a young lady with a bed-ridden Pa. Which Pa, lies a-bed in a bow-window where he can see the ships sail up and down the river.

The house with the bow-window, I thought very well of. If you should want to slip Tom, Jack or Richard on board a foreign packet-boat, there he is – ready.

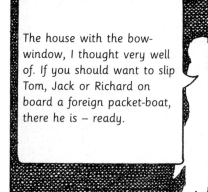

Mr Herbert, by nine o'clock last night housed Tom, Jack or Richard successfully.

When it was dark, I left.

A trip to the theatre worries Pip. Someone is watching him and he knows he has to get the convict out of the country.

When I **struck** down by the river, I found that the spot was anything but easy to find. I came upon the door I wanted. I knocked and Herbert led me into the parlour.

All is well.

Dear boy!

I told him that my chambers had been watched and what Wemmick had said about getting him abroad.

We could take him down the river ourselves when the right time comes. No boat would then be hired and no boatmen; that would save a chance of suspicion.

It might be a good thing if you began to keep a boat and were in the habit of rowing up and down the river.

I set myself to get the boat. I began to go out sometimes alone, sometimes with Herbert.

I could not get rid of the **notion** of being watched.

struck – walked
notion – idea

It was an unhappy life that I lived. One evening I thought I would go to the theatre. The piece was the comic Christmas panto.

I detected Mr Wopsle staring in my direction.

I came out of the theatre afterwards and found him waiting for me.

Mr Pip! I saw you. But who else was there?

He went out. I saw him go.

Remember when you were a child and some soldiers came to chase after two convicts. We came up with the two in a ditch. One of those two prisoners sat behind you tonight. The one who had been **mauled**.

mauled – beaten

Compeyson behind me 'like a ghost'.

An account of a murder makes Pip think of Estella.

I had again left my boat at the **wharf** and was strolling along when a hand was laid upon my shoulder.

Come and dine with me. Wemmick's coming.

Dinner was served.

Miss Havisham wants to see you.

Molly, how slow you are today!

A certain action of her fingers arrested my attention. I had seen such eyes and such hands very lately! I felt absolutely certain that this woman was Estella's mother.

We took our leave early.

That housekeeper? Tell me her story.

Years ago, that woman was tried for murder, and was **acquitted**. Mr Jaggers worked the case. She was under suspicion of having destroyed her child.

Do you remember the sex of the child?

A girl.

wharf – dock
acquitted – found to be innocent

49

Miss Havisham regrets what she has done. Pip rescues her from a fire.

I went down again by coach next day. Miss Havisham was sitting close before the fire.

This is **an authority** to pay you that money to lay out for your friend.

Is she married?

Yes.

It was a needless question

Until you spoke to her the other day, and until I saw you in a looking-glass that showed me what I once felt myself, I did not know what I had done.

What have I done? What have I done!

I stole her heart away and put ice in its place.

If you knew all my story.

I do know your story.

Whose child was Estella? You don't know?

Mr Jaggers brought her here. I wanted a little girl to love and save from my fate.

an authority – an instruction

50

We parted. I called to the woman who had opened the gate that I would walk round the place before leaving.

I looked into the room where I had left her.

I saw a great flaming light spring up. I saw her running at me, fire blazing about her.

I had a great-coat on, and over my arm another. I got them off, threw her down and got them over her. Both my hands were burnt.

She had received serious hurts. By the surgeon's directions, her bed was carried into that room and laid upon the great table.

Estella was in Paris. The surgeon would write to her by the next post.

Herbert was the kindest of nurses. Neither of us spoke about the boat, but we both thought to make my recovery of the use of my hands, a question of so many hours, not of so many weeks.

In his own careful lawyer's way, Mr Jaggers confirms what Pip knows about Estella's parents.

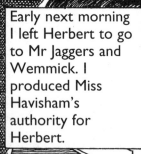

Early next morning I left Herbert to go to Mr Jaggers and Wemmick. I produced Miss Havisham's authority for Herbert.

I did ask Miss Havisham to give me some information relative to her adopted daughter.

I know her mother. I know her father too. Provis – from New South Wales.

He has no belief that his daughter is in existence.

I made an appeal to him to be frank and open with me.

I'll put a case to you. Mind! I admit nothing.

Put the case that a woman held her child concealed, and was obliged to communicate the fact to her legal adviser.

At the same time he held a trust to find a child for an eccentric rich lady to adopt and bring up. Here was one pretty child who could be saved. The legal adviser had this power.

The woman was cleared. When she was set at liberty, she was scared and went to him to be sheltered.

The secret was still a secret, except that you got wind of it. Would you reveal the secret?

Pip and Herbert put their escape plan for the convict into action. But things go wrong!

It was one of those March days when the sun shines hot and the wind blows cold. We went on board and cast off. We intended to row until dark.

The steamer for Hamburg and the steamer for Rotterdam would start from London at about nine. We would **hail** the first.

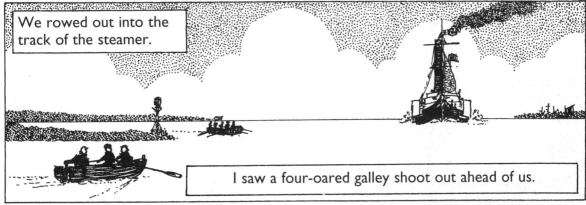

We rowed out into the track of the steamer.

I saw a four-oared galley shoot out ahead of us.

You have a returned Transport there, Abel Magwitch. I call upon him to surrender.

hail – call

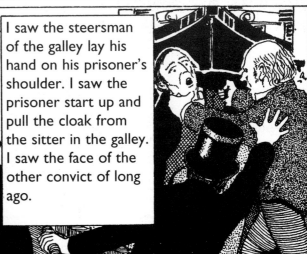

I saw the steersman of the galley lay his hand on his prisoner's shoulder. I saw the prisoner start up and pull the cloak from the sitter in the galley. I saw the face of the other convict of long ago.

I felt the boat sink from under me.

I was taken on board the galley. I saw Magwitch swimming. He was taken and **manacled.**

Magwitch had received some severe injury in the chest.

He did not say what he might have done to Compeyson.

He lay in prison very ill. I saw him every day. The trial came. It was impossible to do otherwise than find him Guilty, the punishment being Death.

manacled – handcuffed

The daily visits I could make him were shortened. Sometimes he was quite unable to speak. He lay, breathing with great difficulty.

You had a child once, whom you loved and lost. She lived and found powerful friends. She is living now. She is a lady and very beautiful. And I love her!

He raised my hands to his lips. Then his head dropped quietly on his breast.

Pip is ill but he realises that true friends never let you down. He decides to go home but another surprise is in store for him!

I was in debt and falling very ill. I had a fever. After I had turned the worst point of my illness I opened my eyes and looked upon the face of Joe.

Is it Joe?

Which it air, old chap.

You break my heart! Don't be so good to me.

Pip, old chap, you and me was ever friends. When the news of your being ill were brought by letter, 'Go to him,' Biddy say.

I **deferred** asking about Miss Havisham until next day.

She ain't living.

What became of her property?

Tied it up on Miss Estella, leaving a cool four-thousand to Mr Matthew Pocket because of Pip's account of him.

The only good thing I had done.

I got up in the morning and Joe was not here. I found a letter.

Not wishful to intrude I have departed fur you are well again dear Pip and will do better without.
Jo
PS Ever the best of friends.

Enclosed in the letter was a receipt for the debt.

deferred – put off   **Tied it up on** – Left it to

What remained for me now, but to follow him to the dear old forge? I would go to Biddy. I would say to her, 'If you tell me you will go through the world with me, you will make it a better world and me a better man.'

After three days I went down to the old place. Joe and Biddy stood before me, arm in arm.

It's my wedding-day, and I am married to Joe!

Dear Biddy, you have the best husband in the whole world.

And, dear Joe, you have the best wife.

I am going abroad and shall never rest until I have worked for the money with which you have kept me out of prison.

Tell me, both, that you can forgive me!

God knows as I forgive you, if I have anythink to forgive!

Amen! And God knows I do.

I sold all I had and joined Herbert. Many a year went round before I was a partner but I lived happily with Herbert and his wife. We worked for our profits, and did very well.

Pip goes to see Joe and Biddy. He meets Estella again in the ruins of Satis House.

For eleven years I had not seen Joe nor Biddy when, upon an evening in December, I laid my hand softly on the latch of the old kitchen door.

There sat Joe, and there was – I again!

We give him the name of Pip for your sake.

Pip, have you forgotten her?

I have forgotten nothing. But that poor dream has all gone by.

Nevertheless, I knew when I said those words that I secretly intended to revisit the old house that evening, for Estella's sake.

I had heard of her being separated from her husband, who had used her with great cruelty. I had heard of the death of her husband some two years before. For anything I knew, she was married again.

There was no house now but the wall of the old garden. I beheld a solitary figure.

Estella!

Do you often come back?

I have never been here since. The ground belongs to me.

Is it to be built on?

At last it is. I came here to take leave of it before its change.

I have often thought of you.

You have always held your place in my heart.

I little thought that I should take leave of you in taking leave of this spot.

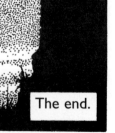
I took her hand in mine and we went out of the ruined place; the evening mists were rising and I saw the shadow of no parting from her.

The end.